FIRST DOG FALA

To Sarge and Rocky, best friends forever,
and to their moms and dad, Shirley, Mike, and Jessica
—E. A. V.

For my loyal friends Kip, Kodaboy, and Nike
—M. G. M.

Ω

Published by
PEACHTREE PUBLISHERS, LTD.
1700 Chattahoochee Avenue
Atlanta, Georgia 30318-2112
www.peachtree-online.com

Text © 2008 by Elizabeth Van Steenwyk
Illustrations © 2008 by Michael G. Montgomery

Book design by Michael G. Montgomery, cover design by Loraine M. Joyner
Composition by Melanie McMahon Ives
Illustrations created in oil on canvas; title created in Adobe Illustrator based on Nick Curtis's
StonyIsland NF; text typeset in Goudy Infant; Afterword typeset in Monotype Imaging's Gil
Sans.

Printed in China
10 9 8 7 6 5 4 3 2 1
First Edition

Library of Congress Cataloging-in-Publication Data

Van Steenwyk, Elizabeth.
  First dog fala / written by Elizabeth Van Steenwyk ; illustrated by Michael G. Montgomery.--
1st ed.
      p. cm.
  ISBN-13: 978-1-56145-411-2 / ISBN-10: 1-56145-411-7
  1. Fala (Dog)--Juvenile literature. 2. Roosevelt, Franklin D. (Franklin Delano), 1882-1945--
Juvenile literature. 3. Dogs--United States--Biography. I. Montgomery, Michael, 1952- II.
Title.
  E807.1.V36 2008
  973.917092--dc22
                                    2008004561

FIRST DOG FALA

Elizabeth Van Steenwyk

Illustrated by Michael G. Montgomery

PEACHTREE
ATLANTA

PRESIDENT FRANKLIN D. ROOSEVELT lived and worked in the White House in Washington, D.C. His days were filled with meetings and telephone calls. But when evening came, his secretaries and advisors hurried home to their own families. His children were grown and gone, and Mrs. Roosevelt traveled frequently on speaking tours.

So at night, the president was often alone.

In 1940, his cousin Margaret Suckley brought him a special present.

"I've got a gift for you, Franklin," she said. "Now you won't be lonely any more." Then she placed a small black Scottish terrier in his arms. The puppy wagged his stubby tail. His dark, round eyes gleamed as he licked the president's chin. The president roared with laughter. It was love at first lick.

The president named the puppy Murray the Outlaw of Fala Hill, after one of his Scottish ancestors. But that was a big name for a little dog, so he called him Fala. Fala didn't go to live with the president immediately. He stayed with Margaret for a few months while she trained him so he could live at the White House and travel with the president. Sometimes he visited the president at his home in Hyde Park, New York.

In November, the president traveled to Hyde Park to vote in the national elections. He and his family stayed up late to listen to the results. When the votes were counted, Roosevelt became the first United States president to win a third term. The next day, neighbors came to congratulate him. Fala greeted everyone, especially the children, by sitting up and barking. Soon after that, Fala came to live with the president at the White House.

The president and Fala kept a regular schedule. In the mornings, Arthur Prettyman, the president's assistant, pushed Roosevelt's wheelchair to the Oval Office. Many years earlier, the president had been sick with a disease called polio that left his legs weak. He had to wear braces and could only walk a few steps at a time. Fala rode in the president's lap.

As they rolled through the halls, three bells sounded throughout the White House to alert everyone that President Roosevelt was moving from one place to another. Fala barked so that everyone knew he was moving too.

When the weather was warm and sunny, the little black Scottie played outdoors in his own fenced-in yard. Now and then, the president looked up from his paper-strewn desk, through the tall windows, over the hedges, and into the garden to watch his dog. He smiled as the puppy chased birds and butterflies.

On rainy days, Fala stayed in the Oval Office, playing with his squeaky rubber doll or with senators and cabinet members who came to see the president. Sometimes the visitors didn't pay enough attention to him. Then Fala whistled through his nose until they scratched his back or threw a ball for him to chase across the office.

At the end of a long day, Arthur Prettyman wheeled the president back to the private quarters of the White House with Fala tippity-tapping beside them. If President Roosevelt didn't have to attend a special dinner in the state dining room, he usually dined alone with his best friend. Someone once asked him what he liked for dinner.

"Whatever Fala likes," the president answered.

President Roosevelt often spoke directly to the American people, in speeches called "fireside chats" that were broadcast over the radio. On December 29, Arthur Prettyman wheeled him into the diplomatic reception room of the White House. There, the president sat before a desk cluttered with microphones and talked about the war in Europe and the economy at home. Cabinet members, the president's mother, and movie stars Clark Gable and Carole Lombard crowded into the small space.

Fala couldn't come since he wouldn't promise to be quiet.

ON JANUARY 20, 1941, President Roosevelt waited in the backseat of a limousine to leave for his inauguration. Fala hopped in too.

"We can't have you barking while the president is talking," said a Secret Service man to Fala. He picked him up.

"Some folks might like his speech better than mine," the president said, laughing.

The limousine drove away without Fala.

Soon after the president began his third term, Fala began to take little trips around town all by himself, never revealing how he'd escaped. One day the Secret Service men found him trotting down F Street. On another trip, he was caught again.

"He went to the Treasury Department this time," said the Secret Service man.

"He must have gone there to get his pay-check," answered the president, smiling.

Summer ended and the pace at the White House picked up. Lights burned late in the Oval Office as diplomats and the president's advisors hurried in and out. Doctors came and went too, for the president, already in poor health, grew more tired and lost weight. He needed rest, but there seemed to be no time for that. Even Fala had trouble getting the president to stop for a game of ball toss.

On December 7, 1941, Japan bombed Pearl Harbor in Hawaii and the United States entered World War II. Fala listened as people talked about the surprise attack in which many American ships were destroyed and thousands of people died.

Inside the White House, the mood was sad. The president signed a law sending seven million American men into battle. People spoke in whispers and hugged each other a lot. Mrs. Roosevelt told newspaper reporters that only Fala's stocking would hang by the White House fireplace for the Christmas holidays. Their sons had gone to war as well.

On December 22, Winston Churchill, the British prime minister, came to visit. The mood in the White House grew a little cheerier. Churchill and Roosevelt had become friends, and they enjoyed listening to each other's stories. Fala listened as well, thumping his stubby tail on the floor when the two men laughed. On Christmas Eve they stood outside on the south portico to view the giant tree glowing with light. The two men wore suits; Fala wore a red bow.

Although he was exhausted, President Roosevelt knew he had to keep up national morale by appearing before the public. So, traveling by train, he visited defense plants around the country. The president's whereabouts were supposed to be top secret until he arrived at his destination, but Fala's presence always gave them away. When the train stopped, Arthur Prettyman walked Fala on the station platform. Then people saw the little black dog and knew that the president was on board. The Secret Service men began to call Fala "The Informer."

April 7, 1944, seemed like any other day, but when Fala entered the Oval Office, people were scurrying around, whispering and giggling. What was going on? Suddenly, reporters and photographers burst into the room. Then the door to the secretary's office opened and Margaret Suckley carried in a birthday cake with four candles on it.

"Happy Birthday, Fala," she said. Everyone began to sing while she lit the candles on the cake. "These folks want to take your picture while you're eating a piece of cake," she told Fala.

The president leaned forward in his chair. "Go on, Fala," he said. "Everyone's waiting."

Fala looked at his cake. He looked at all the faces circling him. Then he backed away. No crumbs for the camera. Not a bite. Not a nibble. He stared at the cake.

Finally, the photographers left. As soon as the door closed and nearly everyone had gone, Fala bit off a chunk of his cake. The president laughed so hard that he had to take off his glasses and wipe his eyes. For a few minutes he forgot his worries about the war.

In early June, the president seldom went to bed and neither did Fala. He tippity-tapped back and forth in the Oval Office, waiting with everyone else for the president.

At noon on June 6, 1944, Fala joined two hundred reporters to listen to Roosevelt announce that American troops had landed on the beaches of Normandy, France. If the invasion succeeded, victory in Europe was assured. Excitement filled the air and Fala could sense it. He barked loudly as he and the president faced the reporters. While they peppered the president with questions about the invasion, Fala wiggled on the couch, then jumped down to race around the room.

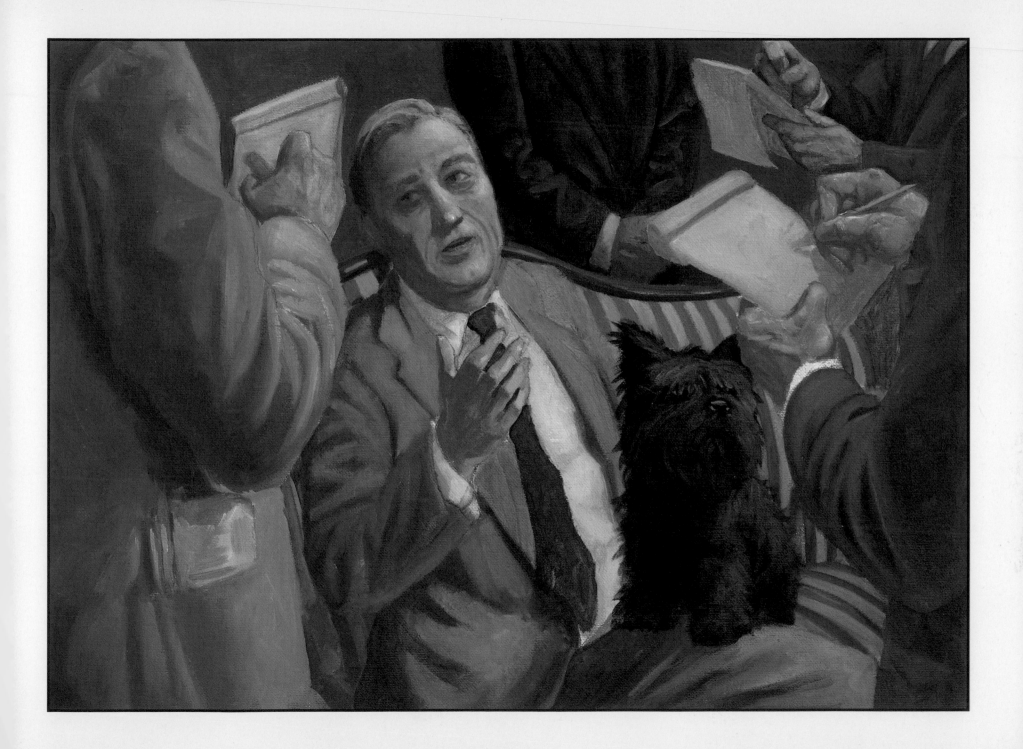

That fall, Roosevelt needed to talk with the country's military leaders in the Pacific. On the way to Hawaii to meet General Douglas MacArthur, the president rested while Fala played ball with the sailors on the ship. He enjoyed his new friends until they cut bits of hair from his back to send home as souvenirs!

Roosevelt was running for a fourth term as president. When he returned from his trip to the Pacific, the press reported that Fala had been left behind on an island and that the president sent a destroyer to retrieve him, costing the taxpayers millions of dollars. President Roosevelt had fun with this story. In a speech, he said, "Well, of course, I don't resent attacks, and my family doesn't resent attacks, but Fala does resent them."

DURING THE LAST FEW WEEKS before the election, the president campaigned hard, ignoring his failing health. He was elected to run the country for four more years.

In April 1945, Roosevelt and Fala went to Warm Springs, Georgia, where the president had a vacation home. The president relaxed and visited with friends, telling them how he looked forward to seeing the return of all American servicemen at war's end.

But that was not to be. The president died suddenly on April 12, 1945, one month before the war ended in Europe. A few days after his death, family and friends gathered in Hyde Park for the funeral. The nation mourned him, but no one missed him more than Fala. He sat beside Mrs. Roosevelt and, when the rifles fired a last salute across the president's grave, Fala howled mournfully.

He had to tell everyone that he'd lost his best friend.

The inscription on the memorial reads:

THEY (WHO) SEEK TO ESTABLISH
SYSTEMS OF GOVERNMENT BASED ON
THE REGIMENTATION OF ALL HUMAN
BEINGS BY A HANDFUL OF INDIVIDUAL
RULERS... CALL THIS A NEW ORDER.
IT IS NOT NEW AND IT IS NOT ORDER

AFTERWORD

Fala lived with Mrs. Roosevelt until his death in 1952. He was

buried at the foot of the sundial in the rose garden near

President Roosevelt's grave. The president said he wanted his

best friend near him for all time. He got his wish.